Selections from

Burgmüller Studies

Opus 100 and 109
Piano Solos

CONTENTS

Art Design: Joann Carrera
Artwork Reproduced on Cover: *A Bend in the River* by Jasper F. Cropsey

JOHANN FRIEDRICH BURGMÜLLER

Born: December 4, 1806, Germany
Died: February 13, 1874, France

Johann Friedrich Burgmüller was born December 4, 1806, near Regensburg, Germany, into a musical family. His father, Johann August Franz, was a prominent organist, teacher, and conductor who founded a musical society in Düsseldorf and the Rhine Music Festival in 1818. This festival continues today as one of the major national music events in Germany. He saw that both of his sons had an interest in music and provided for their musical training beginning at an early age. Johann Friedrich and his brother, Norbert, were both fine musicians, but Norbert was considered much more talented. Unfortunately he died very early, at the age of 26, before establishing himself beyond a circle of friends including other musicians, artists, and poets. He was a relatively unknown figure in society.

Johann Friedrich moved to Paris, France, in 1832 and remained there until his death February 13, 1874. In Paris he was recognized as a fine musician, pianist, and composer. He wrote music there that suited his public, in a lighter style than that of his homeland. Burgmüller is remembered for his salon pieces for piano, songs, and several stage works that include one ballet, but moreso for his collections of piano studies. It is from these volumes that pieces for this new edition were selected. Burgmüller's studies were intended for students and have enough substance that they serve not only as technical exercises, but also as recital pieces. Each study addresses a different technical aspect of piano playing, and all are still used today by teachers around the world.

LA CANDEUR
(Frankness)
Opus 100, No. 1

JOHANN FRIEDRICH BURGMÜLLER

ARABESQUE
Opus 100, No. 2

UNSCHULD
(Innocence)
Opus 100, No. 5

PROGRÈS
(Progress)
Opus 100, No. 6

LE COURANT LIMPIDE
(The Limpid Stream)
Opus 100, No. 7

EL9923

LA GRACIEUSE
(Gracefulness)
Opus 100, No. 8

LA BERGERONNETTE
(The Young Shepherdess)
Opus 100, No. 11

Allegretto

ADIEU
(Farewell)
Opus 100, No. 12

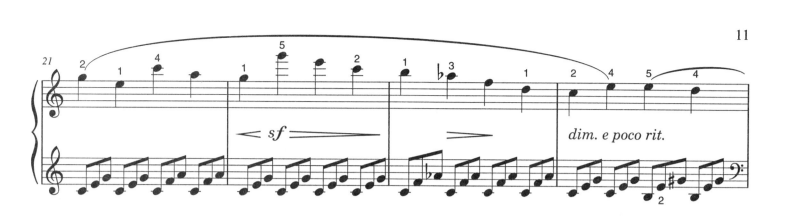

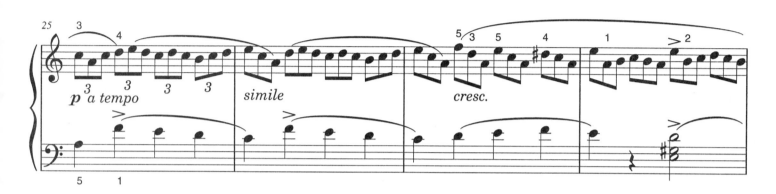

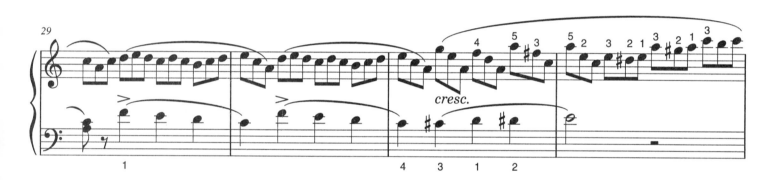

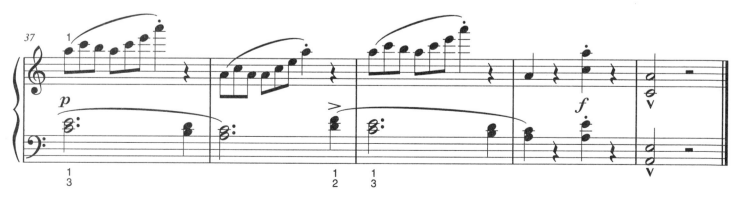

BALLADE
Opus 100, No. 15

Allegro con brio

DOUCE PLAINTE
(Tender Grieving)
Opus 100, No. 16

INQUIÉTUDE
(Discomfort)
Opus 100, No. 18

Allegro agitato

TARANTELLE
Opus 100, No. 20

L'HARMONIE DES ANGES
(Angel Voices)
Opus 100, No. 21

LA CHEVALERESQUE
(The Knight Errant)
Opus 100, No. 25

Allegro marziale

CONFIDENCE
Opus 109, No. 1

LA RETOUR DU PÂTRE
(The Shepherd's Return)
Opus 109, No. 3

AGITATO
Opus 109, No. 8

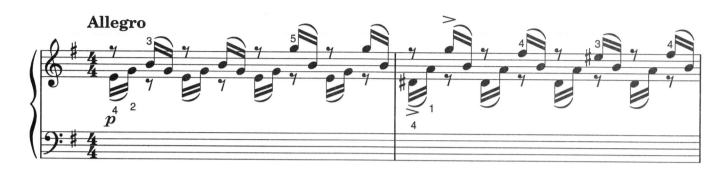

LA CLOCHE DES MATINES
(Morning Bell)
Opus 109, No. 9

Andante sostenuto

LA SÉPARATION
(Parting)
Opus 109, No. 16

BERCEUSE
(Lullaby)
Opus 109, No. 7